Ito

Good ~id to Home

Free Kid

Translated by Cathy Hirano

GECKO PRESS

Not long ago,
my little brother
turned up.

He looks just like a potato.

This is your new brother. His name is Daichan.

Potato-face is always crying.

When he's not crying,
he's eating or pooping.

He's not even
slightly cute.

But for some reason my mother
only cares about him.

She takes no notice of me.

"I guess you don't want
me anymore," I say.
"If you say so, dear."

"I'm going to run away then.
I'll find a new home."
"Yes, dear."

It looks like I really am going.
I pack my most important things.

"This is your last chance to stop me."
"Yes, dear. Here, Daichan — say goodbye
  to your big sister."

"Humph! You'll be sorry!
But don't come crying to me."

Waa!

"Oh dear! Daichan's crying," says my mother.

"What's so great about Daichan?
He's just a lumpy little potato!"

"A cute little potato, though," she says.

Okay, that does it! Goodbye forever!

Be home in time for dinner!

Grrr! Old witchy-poo!

I'm never going back. I'm going
to be the world's cutest stray kid.

Bleh!

Now let's get started.
Ah ha! This gives me an idea.

Where shall I put myself?
Not by the smelly bins!

I'll have to use my best writing.

I don't want people to think I'm stupid.

There! I'm ready for someone to find me.

I wonder what sort of home I'll go to.
I bet it will have a great big yard.

A pool would be nice.

Free Kid

My new father will be handsome and kind,
and my mother will be beautiful and smart.
And I'll be the only one they love.

There'll be lots of servants who call me
"Young Lady" and a driver to take me to
school and back.

Every day after school, I'll invite friends home for amazing parties, and everyone will want to be my best friend.

There won't be a single
potato-faced brother.

In fact, no little brothers allowed!

Hey, someone's coming!

He didn't even look at me.
Probably just as well.

I'm not going off with just anyone.

Only the best is good enough. La-la-la

Here comes another one.

Oops! No other kids! No way!

Don't annoy the little girl, Taku.

Phew! Another close call. I'd rather be a witch's apprentice and stir lizard soup all day than live with a walking potato like that.

Right then, sit up straight. Here comes a
nice-looking woman. She's the one!

Free Kid

Good thing she didn't stop. The nicer
they look on the outside, the more
likely they're a witch on the inside.
She'd probably starve me.

It's okay. I'll be patient.

Someone wonderful is sure to want me.

Hmm. Maybe I don't look special enough just sitting here. I don't want people to think I'm boring.

Free Kid

People probably want a kid who's creative.

Snip, snip

TOM
ATO   Free Kid

43

Okay, how's this for clever?
Toot! Toot! Toot-a-toot-toot!

Toot! Toot! Toot-a-toot-toot!
Free kid anyone?
Toot-a-toot-toot!
Great opportunity!
Toot! Toot! Toot-a-toot-toot!

Toot-toot... Too—

This won't work. No one's going to feel sorry for a kid who's dancing.

I suppose this is better.

"Hello there!"
"Hello, Dog. Are you looking for a cute kid?"

Free Kid

"Okay if I join you? I can't find my
way home. I might need a new one."

"I guess a dog is okay. At least
 you're not a little brother."
"Thank you."

Free Kid

"Woof! This is exciting! I wonder what kind of home we'll end up in?"

"I guess it'll have a big yard where I can run around all day, and a pond wide enough that I can race the fish with my world-beating dog paddle. And no one will yell if I come inside with muddy paws..."

"and there'll be lots of cute kids."

"Nope! No kids! The only kid in that family
 will be me."
"Really? Why?"
"Because I said. And no means no."
"Okay, okay. I get it. No other kids then."
"I'll bring friends you can play with instead."

"Okay, then I can play with your friends,
eat heaps of meat, and sleep in a big soft
bed. How does that sound?"
"It sounds a bit much to ask for."
"You think so?"

"Don't forget, I'm the star. You're just
 an extra."
"All right, all right."
"Hey, someone's coming! Look super cute."
"I'll try."

"Too bad. He looked pretty rich."
"Don't blame me! We might have to
go where there are more people."

"Maybe you're right. But where?"
"Meow. Why not try in front of the station?"
"Hey, good idea! Thank you, Kitty!"

"You're welcome, little girl. May I join you?"
"You do know we're strays, don't you?"

Free Kid
+ Dog

"I do know. I've been watching you.
I'm a stray, too. I've always hoped
someone would take me home.
So if you wouldn't mind..."

"You're pretty dirty though."
"Can you overlook that for now?
I've lived on the street all my life."

"I guess a kitty is okay. At least
  you're not a little brother. Hop in."
"Yippee! At last I can wash my paws
  of being a stray."

"Me—ow. How exciting! I wonder who'll take me home. I hope they'll be kind and give me tasty food and a nice warm place to sleep."

"Is that all you want, Kitty?"
"Sure. I'm just a stray, so that's
    plenty for me."

"Oh, there is one more thing. It might be asking too much, but if no one scolded me for sharpening my claws on the furniture, that would be perfect."

"Actually, that might be too much to ask.
We probably shouldn't be too picky."

"Well, here we are!"
"There are plenty of people.
 It's a great spot for strays."
"Someone's bound to take us soon."

"Right, everyone. Put on your cutest face!"

Free Kid
+ Dog & Kitty

Huff-puff

Free Kid
+Dog & Kitty

Huff-puff
Huff-puff

"May I join you guys?"
"Er..."

"...?"

"...?"

"...?"

"So, Turtle, what kind of home are you after?"

"All I need is a nice aquarium."

"Although, if possible, it should be kept at 25 degrees Celsius, with the water changed every three days. Waterplants and stones would be nice, too. And raw beef for my meals."

Free Kid
+ Dog & Kitty + Turtle

"Whoa! That sounds like a lot of work."
"Not at all. It's really easy to care for a turtle. As long as my home isn't crowded. All I need is a warm place to sun myself. And a cool shady spot. Other than that, there's just my diet to take care of. Besides beef, I need worms, fish and shrimp. Live, of course."

"Look over here! A stray turtle."
"So it is. That's pretty cute!"
"Can I have it? Please?"
"Doesn't it belong to that little girl?"

Free Kid
+ Dog & Kitty + Turtle

"No, no. I'm a bona fide stray."
"See! It doesn't belong to anyone.
Can I take it?"

"I suppose, if you want it very badly.
But you'll have to look after it."
"I will! Hey there, Turtle, you can come
with me."

"Turtle found a home before us. Wowff."
"Meww. I'm a little jealous."
"Who'd want to go with that little boy,
  though? He'll treat Turtle like a toy,
  to chuck out when he gets tired of it."

"Turtle will be sorry. You'll see."
" ... "
" ... "

"My, aren't you a skinny kitty. Do you
belong to this little girl?"
"No, I'm a stray."
"Really? Would you like to come home with
me then? My house is a bit messy, so you
can relax and make yourself comfortable."

Free Kid
+ Dog & Kitty

"Will you feed me?"
"Of course."
"Is there a warm place to sleep?"
"Toasty warm."
"I'm all yours!"

"Wowff..."
"Kitty found a home, too."

"Look! Kitty's coming back."
"I knew it! I bet that woman
  is a mean old witch in disguise."

"She says I can sharpen my claws on the furniture. Her house is so old she doesn't care! Thanks to you, my dream has come true!"
"Sounds like it..."

" ... "

" ... "

Free Kid
Dog & Kitty & ~~Turtle~~

\I / /

"I guess I feel a bit jealous, do you?"
"Yeah."

"Hey Dog, what kind of home
did you have before?"
"Ordinary. Just a small house
and a nice owner."

"But the other day, he got a pet bird.
  He forgot all about me, so I pretended
  to run away."
"I know how you feel."

"But then I got lost. So I thought
I'd better try to find a new home."
"I see."

"It's not easy to find one though, is it?"
"You're right. It's not."

"Hey! Koro! Is that you?"
"Ruff-ruff."
"Where've you been? I was so
  worried about you."
"I'm sorry. I lost my way."

"Is that what happened? And
this little girl took care of you."
" ... "
"Thank you, dear."

I'm so glad!

TOM
ATO

Free Kid
+Dog & ~~Kitty~~ ~~+Turtle~~

"Come on, Koro. Let's go home. Say
goodbye to the little girl. The others
will be excited to see you."
"Ruff-ruff!"

"..."

Pah! Traitor! But I won't give up.
Why shouldn't I find a nice new home...?

With parents who love me, and only me.

With servants and a driver and
lots of friends who think I'm great.

With no little potato-faced brother.

Yup. That kind of home...

"..."

"Look! There's a very cute free kid over here."
"So there is. She'd make a perfect sister for Daichan."
"She certainly would. We couldn't do better."

"But I wonder if she'd like that.
We should ask her first, don't you think?"

"Absolutely. Let's ask."

"Hi, little girl. We're looking for a sister for our little potato here. Would you like to come home with us?"

So I gave up being a stray kid...

to be a big sister for that little potato.

The end

This edition first published in 2022 by Gecko Press
PO Box 9335, Wellington 6141, New Zealand
info@geckopress.com

English-language edition © Gecko Press Ltd 2022
Translation © Cathy Hirano 2022

Gokigen na Sutego
Written and illustrated by Hiroshi Ito © 1991, 1995
This edition originally published in Japan in 1995
by Tokuma Shoten Publishing Co., Ltd., Tokyo
English-language translation rights arranged
through Japan Foreign-Rights Centre

Distributed in the United States and Canada by Lerner Publishing Group, lernerbooks.com
Distributed in the United Kingdom by Bounce Sales and Marketing, bouncemarketing.co.uk
Distributed in Australia and New Zealand by Walker Books Australia, walkerbooks.com.au

Gecko Press is committed to sustainable practice. We publish books to be read over and over.
We use sewn bindings and high-quality production and print all our new books using
vegetable-based inks on FSC-certified paper from sustainably managed forests.

Edited by Penelope Todd
Design and typesetting by Katrina Duncan
Printed in China by Everbest Printing Co. Ltd,
an accredited ISO 14001 & FSC-certified printer

ISBN hardback: 978-1-776574-42-1
ISBN paperback: 978-1-776574-51-3
Ebook available

For more curiously good books, visit geckopress.com

Gecko Press is a small-by-choice,
independent publisher of children's books
in translation. We publish a curated list
of books from the best writers
and illustrators in the world.

Gecko Press books celebrate unsameness.
They encourage us to be thoughtful and inquisitive,
and offer different—sometimes challenging, often
funny—ways of seeing the world. They are printed
on high-quality, sustainably sourced paper with
stitched bindings so they can be read and re-read.

For more Gecko Press illustrated chapter books,
visit our website or your local bookstore.
You might like...

Yours Sincerely, Giraffe by Megumi Iwasa
and Jun Takabatake, in which pen pals Penguin
and Giraffe become confused, because it's hard
to imagine someone you've never seen.

My Happy Life by Rose Lagercrantz and Eva Eriksson,
a book about best friends and life in the world
of Dani, who has a special ability to be happy
and make those around her happy too.

Detective Gordon: The First Case by Ulf Nilsson and
Gitte Spee, for detective stories set in a friendly
forest, where Detective Gordon seeks justice for
all and always makes time for delicious cakes.

A Bear Named Bjorn by Delphine Perret, for readers
who enjoy a gentle bushwalk with an observant bear.